COME TO BED WITH MOTHER

J.D. WILLIAMS

SWEETSPIRE LITERATURE
MANAGEMENT

TABLE OF CONTENTS

OTHER BOOKS WRITTEN BY J.D. WILLIAMS

A TRILOGY OF CRIME

"WHERE'S HENRY?" - DETECTIVE
AND INTERNATIONAL CRIME

THAILAND TRIANGLE - DETECTIVE
AND INTERNATIONAL CRIME

FULL CIRCLE - DETECTIVE AND INTERNATIONAL CRIME

A TRILOGY OF SIENCE FICTION

THE PILGRIMS OF GLIESE - SCIENCE FICTION

END GAME - SCIENCE FICTION

DESTRUCTION OF THE ORION NEBULA - SCIENCE FICTION

IN PURSUIT OF THE INNOCENT

I WOULDN'T CHANGE A THING

ACKNOWLEDGEMENT

I want to thank my wife for encouragement to write.

CHAPTER ONE

THE ARRIVAL

Brenda needed a drink, she was looking for a place to park her 1954 Buick, it had 150,000 miles, and was running like shit, she figured it would kick the bucket any day now, spotted a corner bar on the main street, and as this was an upscale part of town figured it would be safe to get a drink, licked her lips and speaking to no-one in particular,"I need a drink real bad, Pattie's looks safe,I'll have something to eat, and a few drinks, and maybe hook up with somebody for the afternoon."

Brenda had just left the lawyers office, and signed the final divorce papers, her ex-husband was a son of a bitch, he had probably screwed twenty or thirty women in the fifteen years of marriage. She had ignored his philandering for the sake of their thirteen year old daughter, but when the creep came home, and gave her the clap, that was too much. She filed for a divorce. Her husband went berserk. He tried to blame her for giving him the venereal disease.

"You always were a slut, I'll bet you were screwing the next door neighbor I saw how you looked at him, that's how I got the clap, not the other way around you want to divorce me, Hell when my lawyer gets through with you, your name will be shit, and if you think your going to get alimony you are nuts!!"He grabbed a baseball bat and threatened to beat her brains in."I'll kill you bitch, your brains will be splattered all over the frigging wall, ha, ha." she fled to the bathroom, and locked the door,after a couple of hours in the bathroom, everything went silent, she slowly opened the door and peeked out. Her husband was nowhere to be found.

Brenda wandered around the house in a daze, she noticed   a bottle of whiskey sitting on the kitchen counter, opened the kitchen cabinet, and reached for a water glass sat it on the counter, poured it full of whiskey, sat down on a stool, and started to sip the nectar pondering her next move, the whiskey calmed her nerves thinking that was good,"I will have another glass."She drank more whiskey, and instead of calming her as she wished, the fear vanished. Now she wanted vengeance,"I should kill the lying son of a bitch, maybe cut his heart out."

Brenda `started slurred her words, she opened the kitchen drawer, reached in, and her hand slowly wrapped around a butcher knife, she started to laugh, tears ran down her cheeks, she had the crying drunks.

"I have to cut off his manhood, castrate the scum, he has bought me nothing, but misery since I married him." Walking unsteadily with the butcher knife in her hand, slowly opened the bedroom door, there he was laying on the bed half drunk, his privates hanging out of his shorts. The sight was almost too much to bear. Brenda raised the knife, and entered the bedroom thinking,"I have to make him pay for all the years of humiliation he has put me through, at last I will have my revenge."

She walked quietly to the bed, reached down, and grabbed his testicles, she brought down the butcher knife. Luck or not he was only resting, when he felt someone grab his jewels, he jumped out of bed with a cut on his left testicle screaming,"You crazy bitch, I'll have you put away for ten years for attempted murder."

He barreled out of the bedroom door knocking the knife from her hand, ran into the living room, picked up the phone, and called the police,"Help me, help me, my wife tried to kill me."

He opened up the cut, and rubbed blood on his shorts and down his leg by the time Brenda snapped out of her reverie the police came in the door, threw her to the floor, she was handcuffed, and dragged to jail where she spent the night. Her mother bailed her out the next morning,"Brenda what were you thinking, trying to kill your husband, he is a good man",her mother said.

Brenda"He's a no good cheating son of a bitch, he gave me the clap because he couldn't keep his dick in his pants."she retorted. A week later Brenda received a letter from her husbands lawyer he was filing for a divorce.

Her husband's lawyer convinced him not to press charges, but use the attack in the divorce as leverage, threaten to press charges, and let the ex take responsibility for the daughter. He would be home free.

Brenda had made a major mistake, Arnold would hold this over her head forever he had promised not to press charges if she didn't ask for alimony because if she did he threatened to take custody of their daughter

Sara,and file attempted murder charges. She could possibly receive five to ten years for attempted murder.

All the bastard had to pay was twenty dollars a week until his daughter was eighteen years old, and he was home free. If it wasn't for her daughter, she wished she had killed the fucking scum bag, thinking,"I would have loved to see him bleed to death."

CHAPTER TWO

REFLECTION

Brenda was a petite five foot two, weight one hundred ten pounds, blue eyes, her hair was shiny auburn, she was sporting a pair of red short, shorts, a tight pullover that revealed skin from the bust to her belly button in other words at thirty five she still turned heads she had been in this mode ever since she had been released from jail. She was psychologically trying to prove to herself, that she was still a woman who could turn heads. The trauma her husband had put her through had seriously made her doubt herself. As Brenda pulled up to the parking space, she saw the opening could fit at least two or three cars, she always had trouble backing up so this was the "Cats Meow" opening the car door made sure if there was any man in sight he would have no trouble missing her exit from the car standing up straight, puffing out her chest, fluffing out her long auburn hair she stood there for a couple of seconds looking into her compact mirror figured if anyone was looking they would get an eye full as she strutted across the street, and pushed open the Pub's double doors. Walked into the Pub's cool interior, looking around for a good place to sit, some ofthe booths were occupied, glancing toward the bar saw only one seat was filled, thinking the bar looked more appealing.

Brenda walked to the end of the bar it was as long as the serving area, and the booths, she thought,"let me sit my pretty little ass here, I'll be at least ten seats from the nearest customer."

Tim the bartender who didn't miss anything, glanced down the bar at the pretty miss, when she had walked into the bar he had followed her with his eyes as she settled into her seat. Tim, who was a hound dog in his own right, sauntered over to Brenda and asked her,"What will you have little lady?"She answers,"give me a double bourbon on the rocks with a splash of soda."Tim answered."No problem miss coming right up, are you waiting for someone?"

Brenda took a second or two to answer,"No, I just want a little time to myself, I just finalized a divorce."

That perks Tim's ears up, just finalized a divorce, they were key words."Yes miss coming right up."

Brenda sat sipping on her drink in a kind of reverie, when she saw the Pub door open, sunlight spread over the bar, and out of the corner of her eye she spots this hunk walking in, about six feet two, two hundred ten pounds, nicely built. As he walked to the bar Tim gives him a head signal toward the woman at the end of the bar. Tim knew Dick as he was a regular customer. He caught the signal immediately, not to be conspicuous he sits three seats down from Brenda, and orders a Schlitz draft.

Tim placed the beer in front of Dick, and gives him a look that said, "Try the redhead at the end of the bar." Tim and Dick chatted for a few minutes, Dick turned to look at Brenda,"can I buy you a drink? You look lonely." Dick said. Brenda looks up answering,"Why not."

The bartender placed an upside down shot glass in front of Brenda signifying when she finished her drink,another was forth coming, after the shot glass was placed, Dick quietly asked."Do you mind if I sit closer, and maybe we can talk."Brenda answers without thinking,"No problem,we can get drunk together."

Dick picked up his drink, and moved his stool right next to her, the smell of his pheromones were like a brick bat against her psyche she thinks,"God what in the hell am I doing?"

The draw was more than she could stand, she had not been with a man since that needle dick the bed bug fucker had given her the clap, and during the divorce didn't want him to have anything more to hang over her head. So she stayed away from sex with men or women.

Dick and Brenda chatted for awhile, and all the time they were talking her short shorts were riding up her crotch, she wasn't wearing underwear, and she kept it shaved. The sensation was literally driving her nuts. Dick sensed she was a score. Brenda downed the second bourbon, and asked Dick,"Do you live around here?"

She was low on funds, and needed a sugar daddy. Dick always quick on the trigger answered,"Two blocks I have an apartment."Brenda answered,"Lets go for a walk, I need some fresh air."

They both slipped off of the bar stools simultaneously, and headed for the door. Dick held the door open for Brenda, the sunlight was blinding, Dick took her by the arm, and guided her down the street till her eyes adjusted to the sunlight. They walked silently until he pointed to an enclosed doorway.

"This is where I live on the second floor."

Dick put his key in the lock, opened the door, held it open to allow Brenda to start up the stairs ahead of him, he locked the door, and followed behind her at the top of the stairs there were two doors, one facing the rear of the building, and one toward the front.

Dick motioned toward the front door, pushing past Brenda he opened the apartment door. The apartment had three rooms, a combination kitchen/sitting room, a small bedroom, and a larger bedroom, with enough furniture to make the apartment comfortable.

CHAPTER THREE

THE COPULATION

Brenda threw her pocketbook on the couch, and sat down with a sigh!! She was not used to drinking, and everything was a blur, her inhibitions were gone she needed a man, she gazed up at Dick, and asked,"are you clean? I don't need to have sex with a scum bum."

Dick looked askance,"No my package is clean, just broke up with my wife, my ex wife, be not worried."

He walked to the couch, leaned down gave her a kiss, and at the same time gently pulled up her top revealing her firm breasts, and began to rub her nipples. She opened her mouth to accept his tongue she could feel the moisture in her pants, there was a wet spot on the couch, still savoring the kiss pushed him gently away, and whispered,"Not here in the bedroom on the bed."

They left a trail of their clothes on the way to the bedroom, first her sandals, his shoes and pants, her top (no bra), his underwear then they hit the bed. Brenda landed on her back, Dick face down in her possum, he started to caress her with his tongue, she went into immediate climax, as she was climaxing he entered her, and Brenda felt her body shake and quiver, her head felt like the top would blow off. She had never in her life had such pleasurable sex, in thinking back on the years she had spent with her ex- husband, it had been a waste of her life. He had used most of his cream screwing other women.

This could be a coupling made in heaven. Dick had a decent job, and money in the bank. The tryst lasted for at least an hour, they had sex in every position known, and at the end of their Kama Sutra fell asleep in each others arms. They slept for about an hour then Brenda jumped up.

"Dick can I use your phone? I need to call my mother, she is watching my daughter."Brenda dialed the phone, it rang and rang waiting for her mother to answer. Finally, her mother picked up."Hello Mom? could you watch Sara tonight, I'm stuck in the city with a girlfriend."

Her mother answered,"Brenda are you in trouble again?, you know the next time they will put you away."

"Mom please, do you think I am crazy, I am done with that shit."Brenda woke about six am. She took a shower, and borrowed Dicks pants walked to her car, and grabbed a change of clothes. Brenda was a waitress her work day started at eleven in the morning for lunch, she had to look like a nice clean Mom, not a little hottie. She brought the clothes back to Dicks apartment, put on lipstick, a little powder, work shoes, long skirt, bra, blouse, and she was all ready to rock. On her trek to her mothers, Brenda considered her options, stay with her mother and father, let them babysit her daughter, or build a friendship with Dick. She didn't love Dick, but they had a great sexual connection, together they could afford to rent a small house and live a decent life. Dick had given her his phone number and said,"Call anytime."

Brenda wasn't looking for a one night stand, she wanted a stable home for her daughter and herself.

She only stayed at her parents house long enough to make sure her daughter was ready for school, and left to goto work. She looked at the clock in fifteen minutes her shift was over at eight o'clock, she changed out of her waitress uniform, she thought to herself,"I need to get home and put Sara to bed, or my mother will be on my ass. I don't need her giving me grief about not being a good mother."

Traffic was light, so it only took about thirty minutes to reach her parents house. She pulled into the driveway, Brenda slid out of the car, straightened her skirt, checked in the side mirror to make sure her lipstick was OK, and put a little powder on her cheeks. She had been very sexually active the last couple of days, and did not want to hear a sermon from her mother and father as soon as she walked through the door.

Brenda closed the door and walked into the family room. Her father was sitting on the couch with a can of beer in his hand, his feet on the ottoman watching television. Her father was five feet eleven inches tall, two hundred and ten pounds all solid muscle. His hair at fifty nine was turning grey, eyes still a sparkling blue, retired from the police force at fifty eight.

It was an enforced retirement, so now he was a bounty hunter and worked part time as a Private Detective with his somewhat screwy partner, who by the way was his brother in law. Looking up at his daughter,"Who were you shacking up with this time? I hear you picked up a crud at the Pub downtown."Her father said. Brenda stood with her mouth open, this caught her completely off guard, she was utterly speechless, Brenda shot back,"Dad what in the hell are you doing, spying on me?"

Her dad answered,"I used to patrol that neighborhood, and the bartender is an ex cop, he recognized you from a couple of family barbecues we went to. He knows that creep, and he has a pretty shady past, I am going to have my partner, your uncle Frank, check him out."

Brenda blew up,"I don't care what you find out, most of it will be bullshit anyway, you just want a reason to keep me here. I spent fifteen years with that asshole husband, I want to be free of that prison."

Dick was reminiscing,"Brenda's not a bad lay in bed, I didn't delve into her personal life, but shacking up for awhile sure wouldn't put a crimp in my style."

He looked in the mirror and kept shaving, drawing the razor harshly against his chin he smiled thinking,"That little bitch who accused me of rape, I fixed her real good Hiring those two goons for five hundred dollars had paid well, they had silenced her parents by wrecking their car and threatening to kill their elderly mother and father, then they took little Milessa for a ride and told her if she testified they would gut her and her parents."

All of a sudden there was no case, the parents swore that she was home the night Milessa claimed the act was done, and their daughter was prone to exaggerate. The police suspected that the family had been coerced but could not prove it.

CHAPTER FOUR

BACKLASH

Brenda's father said,"I don't care what you want, I am going to have Frank look into this creeps past, I'm trying to protect my grand daughter, and if you are to dumb to see that I am sorry, but I will do what is necessary to protect my family."

Brenda could feel her blood pressure rising, she grabbed her pocketbook from the couch, and on her way out the door shouted to her father,"I think all men are assholes you thought my ex-husband was the cats ass, because he gave you free baseball tickets, all the time you knew he was screwing anything with a crack and you looked the other way because he was a nice guy, screw you and the horse you rode in on."

With that tirade Brenda slammed out of the house, banging the front door so hard her father thought the glass would shatter. Brenda was fuming,"I wonder if Dick is still at his apartment?"

She sat back and thought,"Brenda keep your cool, let him make the first move, don't let your feelings take over like you did with your ex, if you hadn't tried to cut off his genitalia you would be home free."

She took a deep breath, and another deep breath, she could feel her blood pressure going down,"That's it she thought keep calm, don't let Dick know how much you want this, just let him know about the house for rent and ask if he is interested."

Brenda drove around looking for a pay phone, there was one on the corner. She pulled to the curb, parked and exited the car, looked for a dime in her purse, dropped it in the coin slot and slowly dialed Dick's phone number it rang three times and she was about to hang up and Dick answered,"Hello, Dick the man here."

Brenda thought,"That was nice, this is Brenda what do you have going today? I thought you would be on the dredge."

He answered,"no the diesel engine needs repairs, we will probably work over the weekend, how is everything with you?"She held her breath then answered,"pretty good, I saw a house for in the paper a mile or so out of town the rent is one hundred and fifty dollars a month and it includes electric and heat."

Dick looked at the phone thinking,"This broad is a fast worker, she is looking to shack up."It took him by surprise he answered,"I can't promise anything we can look at the house after I do my next tour on the dredge, which is seven days from Friday, will call you when the boat docks."

Brenda thought fast, she didn't want Dick calling her parents house, her father would screw everything up,"Call me at work, if I'm not there just leave a message hopefully the house will still be for rent." She hung up the phone and said to herself,"Now I call my mother, I will have to eat crow, and kiss ass at home after what I said to my father."

CHAPTER FIVE

BACK IN THE GAME:

After he hung up, Dick started to pack for his week on the river the job paid well, and dredging the harbor would last at least a couple more years. Grabbing a few pairs of socks, BVDs, a half a dozen shirts and pants, threw in his razor and shaving cream, stopped himself short should he or shouldn't he, picking up the snub nosed thirty two he had to get rid of it.

Dick broke it down, and wrapped it in an old tee shirt. When the dredge was out in the mouth of the river he would dump it piece by piece. The gun had been stolen, and the story of the gun was the cops could ID it from ballistics he thought,"What ever in the hell that meant?"

He picked up his duffle, locked the apartment, stood there to make sure he had not forgotten anything, took the steps two at a time, opened the door that put him onto the sidewalk walked three steps to the curb, and waited for his ride.

Sammy drove up fifteen minutes later, Dick opened the car door, and climbed in. Sammy looked over and said,"did you bring it? we have to dump it this tour, the cops are hot to trot for this rod."

Dick replied,"what in the hell are you worried about? when we knocked over the convenience store I popped the Daego on the cranium when he wasn't looking, and we cleaned out the register he never saw what hit him he was out of the hospital in a week, he has not the slightest idea what happened. We can't be identified."

Sammy looking straight ahead quips,"Dick, why don't you shut up, and do what the man wants you to do, just dump the gun no questions asked and forget it."

They drove in silence for thirty minutes. When they arrived Sammy backed the car up against the dock and parked. He looks at Dick,"Let's go chump, and don't screw it up."

Sammy turned off the car, pulled the key out of the ignition switch, swung open the drivers side door exited the car leaving Dick sitting in the passenger seat. He sat there for a few seconds, reaches into the back seat grabs his duffle bag and follows behind Sammy.

He didn't want to screw this job on the dredge up, he was being paid seventy five dollars a week, plus time and a half over forty hours he had been working on the dredge for six months, and once or twice a week they did a pickup. He had never been able to figure out who was in the game, the Captain was never involved in any manner, and the First Mate just looked the other way when he wasn't helping. The registered seamen Todd and Sammy did all the dirty work, every Tuesday and Thursday they would allow the dredge to drift out to the mouth of the Delaware, and pick up a small boat loaded with five or six bundles wrapped in burlap. Todd and Sammy would unload the cargo, and the dredge would head up river, where they would off load the merchandise. The rest of the crew looked the other way, and would never comment on the pickups.

Dick enjoyed the camaraderie, and the good food.

Lunch was good and supper was great, dinner was to die for thick sirloin steaks, baked potatoes, and all the goodies.

He received an extra twenty bucks a week to do as he was told, and keep his mouth shut the crew had worked ten, ten hour shifts, and the crew was itching for shore leave.

Dick had been thinking about Brenda, the more he thought about renting a place and shack up for awhile was sounding pretty good. He had her phone number at the apartment and as soon as the dredge docked, he was going to give her a call. The dredge docked, and as they were leaving Sammy turned to Dick,"How about a ride, and we can do some business?"

Figuring it was code to knock over another store,"I would like to Sammy, but I have personal business to take care of that can't wait",Dick begged off. Sammy gave him a sidelong glance, shrugged,"See you in five days."

RECONCILIATION

As soon as Brenda left Dick she figured she better cozy up to her mother and father, when she called her father answered."Dad this is your daughter, please don't hang up I apologize for the way I acted, you were only thinking of me, and your granddaughter ,is it OK if I come home?"

Her dad gave in immediately saying,"Supper will be on the table when you get here."

She changed out of her waitress uniform, the restaurant had put her on the morning shift that started at six in the morning, and ended at three in the afternoon. The drive to her parents house was uneventful, on her drive to her parents Brenda wondered if Dick's tour on the dredge was over. Little did she know when Dick had settled down in his apartment he had called the restaurant where she worked, and left a message for her to call when she started her next morning shift.

Brenda parked in the driveway, and slowly climbed up the porch steps expecting the usual harassment for not spending enough time with her daughter but to her surprise her father greeted her with a hug and points to the kitchen saying,"dinners ready wash up, we will wait for you."

Her mother had outdone herself, the table was set with roast beef, mashers, a nice salad, and an apple pie. They all sat down to eat when dinner was over they went into the living room, and pulled out a board game. Brenda,her mother and Sara started to play, Brenda's father begged off."I have paper work to do, and a meeting in twenty minutes."

Joe went upstairs to call his brother in law, who was also his partner in the Detective Agency,"Frank this is Joe, do you have anymore information on this Dick character?"Frank answered,"We should meet and go over his folder."Joe agreed,"I will see you at the office in forty five minutes."

He put on a clean pair of pants, pulled on a tan shirt with short sleeves from the closet looked in the mirror to make sure it was buttoned correctly, sat on the bed pulled on a pair of loafers, slipped a pair of suspenders over his broad shoulders snapped them in place, and was all set to go. As he was walking out the door Brenda looked up from the board game and said,"be careful out there"."Joe just kind of grunted,"Will do, see you in a few hours."

He opened the front door, crossed the porch, dismounted the steps stopped at the curb, opened the door to his new Ford, put the key in the ignition. He sat back listening to the purr of the engine, and the new car smell opened a pack of Camels lit up inhaled, and pulled away from the curb."All the while thinking what in the hell has Frank dug up now?"

CHAPTER SEVEN

THE BOMB SHELL

Joe decided to take the parkway. It was after seven, and traffic would be slim to none, it took about thirty minutes to arrive at the office. Joe found a parking place next to the office, he slowly exited the car, walked to the side door leading to their office and rang the bell. Frank buzzed him in immediately he had seen Joe parking.

Joe pushed the door open, and mounted the stairs at a quick pace. I have to keep in shape, he thought to himself, at the top of the landing he turned right, and opened the office door. Frank was sitting behind a large desk with a spot light on his paper work, Joe's partner greeted him,"about time you got here sit down and have a drink you're going to need it."

His partner pulled out a bottle of Rye whiskey, a couple of water glasses, and poured three fingers for both of them. Joe lit up a cigarette took large drag, picked up the glass of Rye raised the glass to his brother in law, touched glasses, and gave the greeting "Salute" and downed the whiskey. Frank started the conversation,"This Dick your daughter is mixed up with seems to be charmed.

He wiggled his way out of a statuary rape charge, word is he hired a couple of goons from down town to harass the parents, and threatened to kill the daughter if she testified. The case was dropped and the parents stonewalled the police stating their daughter was home when the assault happened, and she was prone to imagine things.

Listen to this story, this Dick works on a dredge cleaning out the Delaware River and the local police and the FBI are sure they are running drugs, the dredge has been under surveillance for the last six months. The captain always seems to be in his cabin when the pickups are made, the First Mate gets involved occasionally."

Poor Joe sits there with his mouth half open, the cigarette falls from his mouth, his heart is pounding." Joe you can't tell anyone about this, especially your daughter, it would blow the entire operation. They are sending in an out of area undercover state trooper with seamen's papers to try to piece together where the drugs are coming from, and who is doing the distribution."

He just sat there not believing what he had just heard. Frank his partner took a deep breath and continues,"are you ready for the rest of the story?"

Joe held his head answering,"Let me have it."

He continues,"Dick rides with this dago named Sammy and because of the surveillance on the dredge the police noticed that about once a week for the last two months, an hour or so after the second shift is over, when those two leave the dredge there is a gas station stickup or a convenience store robbery in the suburbs."

He continues,"at the last robbery the store owner was pistol whipped, with a thirty two caliber pistol, the cops found a slug and ballistics tied it to a murder up north in Scranton, it's a pattern."Joe could not keep quiet any longer."Where in the hell did my daughter get hooked up with this asshole? I know I screwed up by not telling her about her ex-husband, and now she doesn't believe anything I say. If this investigation is ongoing I'll have to sweat it out."

Frank started to speak again,"I've had both of these guys checked out. Dick has a couple of things on his record, but nothing earth shaking, an arrest for drunk and disorderly, a bar brawl, both of which he paid fines. Meanwhile this Sammy character has been in and out of prison since he was sixteen, grand theft auto, selling drugs in Philly, threatening, the cops are sure he is mixed up with the mob but haven't been able to nail him yet."Joe cuts Frank short and says,"You know Frank if I push this with Brenda she will be more determined to go with Dick, and if we put pressure on Dick, it is going to give the boys on the dredge something to look over their shoulders about, thinking this is all connected."

Frank picked up the Rye and poured both of them another glass, sat back and stared at Joe asking,"now what my friend? Brenda is right in the middle of this shit storm, I'll do all I can to keep her safe."

Joe just sat for a moment, he knew Frank was one hundred percent right, he would have to pray Brenda saw the light real fast,Joe looked at his partner and said,"You are a real fuck, I think you really enjoyed this scenario." Frank shrugged,"Hey Joe, you asked me to check this schmuck out, and I did my best, com se com sa, what

will be, will be. I'll keep one of our people on him, maybe we can put him away."He rose from his chair, and gave Frank a look that could kill, strode across the office, opened the office door he intended to slam it, but thought better of it and closed the door with a slight click. Joe walking down the stairs thinking,"I hope Brenda gets rid of this asshole real fast, this is one screwed up mess if there ever was one, I don't dare tell her mother she would go nuts."

CHAPTER EIGHT

CO-HABITATION

Unbeknown, to her parents Brenda and Dick had rented a house just outside of Camden, three bedrooms on half an acre, the rent was one hundred seventy five dollars a month, plus utilities. Dick was the same distance from work except he was on the other side of the river, and Brenda had a waitressing job down the street. Sara her daughter would catch a bus on the corner to take her to school.

They combined their furniture, and only needed a few things to complete their household. Dick went to work as usual, but stayed away from Sammy. The last heist when Sammy fired the gun had made him leery. Sammy had come close to offing the store clerk, and he had a crawly feeling down the back of his neck that something was not quite right.

The captain had signed on a new crew member with seamen papers, the new crew member was six foot two inches, two hundred and thirty pounds, he looked like an ex-boxer, square jaw, big chest, blond hair, and fists like hammers.

He had an upstate accent that sounded Polish. His story was he had spent a couple of years on tramp steamers sailing to Europe and Asia. His name was Olof, he kept a low profile, and did his work, he knew his way around the dredge and meshed with the crew.

Dick had a funny feeling about Olof, he didn't know why but there was something about him that didn't ring true, his story was too pat. Olof was getting buddy, buddy with Sammy, and since Dick had distanced himself from Sammy, he was looking for a new partner.

Dick and Brenda were getting settled in Brenda had moved out of her parents house without a goodbye, or leave a forwarding address he was relaxed he had a boy eleven, and a girl eight he had not seen them in eight months.

His ex-wife was a real bitch she was always trying to get him to pay extra for the kids, what a pain in the ass a real trouble maker, as for her collecting support now that he was living in another state good luck, his wife and kids could go screw. Just because he liked rough sex his ex had slapped a restraining order on him, and filed for a divorce. She had cleaned out the bank accounts,had him barred from the house, the only thing he had from the divorce was two suitcases with his clothes sitting on the sidewalk.

He had skated through the underage charges, and the second charge could never be proved, staying clear of Sammy only associating with him on the dredge, he was bad news he felt his luck was turning around for the good. The new crewman had ingratiated himself with the crew, even the Captain took a liking to Olof, he was a hard worker, and didn't mind taking a little skim once in awhile. He kept his mouth shut. Dick felt something wasn't kosher, he thought to himself,"Enough of this shit,I must be getting paranoid."It was early afternoon when Dick pulled into the drive way of the house thinking,"Damn, Brenda was home, I think I'll have a matinee."

He got out of the car, and strode to the house, pushed open the screen door, and there was Brenda in her short, shorts. He greeted her,"Hi babe, let's have a quickie." Brenda replies,"Are you crazy my daughter is due home in twenty minutes."Dick insists,"I want it, and I will get it."said Dick.

He picked her up bodily, turned her facing him, threw her down on the kitchen table pulled her pants down around her ankles, and penetrated her all in one motion.

She tried to get away, but he was to strong she could not move. When he was done, Dick left Brenda lying on the kitchen table with her pants still hanging around her ankles. He walked to the fridge pulled out a can of beer opened it, and looking back over his shoulder saying, "Thanks that made my day."Dick walked into the living room picked up the paper, plopped down on the couch and started reading. Brenda was furious."Who in the hell did he think he was? I am not some whore off the street." She was rearranging her clothes, and getting ready to give Dick a piece of her mind, when her daughter came running into the house greeting her mother,"Hi mom."

Brenda responded,"Did you have a good day at school?" Sara gave her mother a big smile, opened the fridge and grabbed a fudge popsicle. She looked lovingly at her daughter she was blossoming into a mature young lady.

CHAPTER NINE

MISOGYNY AT IT'S PUREST

It was late Saturday night, and Dick had stopped at the local bar he put down a few shots, and beers, thinking to himself,"I have been nice till now, never have had real feelings for women, as far as I am concerned they are here for my pleasure."He had another round, and tried to put the make on the woman sitting next to him at the bar, she told him to get lost. When he left the bar he was drunk, and enraged,"It's time I do what I do."

When he arrived at the house, it was one thirty in the morning he crawled out of the car, steadied himself on the car hood and went straight for the front door,all the time singing a little ditty over and over."It's hot in the summer and It's time for some dicky dunking."

He kept repeating the ditty over, and over. Dick reaching the bedroom pushed open the door, while humming to himself, peeled off his clothes, Brenda looked up still half asleep.

"What in the hell are you doing Dick, it's one thirty in the morning?, you will wake Sara."

Completely ignoring her prostrations, and still humming his little rhyme, before she could move he was on top of her. He pulled off her pajamas, rolled her over and stood her on her knees, and pushed her backwards with her legs under. Brenda tried to fight him off to no avail. He was stronger than ever, he mounted her, and she started to cry in this position she was totally helpless, Dick berated her."Come on bitch give me some movement, and a few moans."

When he is done he looks at Brenda and says."I am just beginning to break you in, I will waste you and your entire fucking family."

Brenda stays silent, remembering her fathers words. "This guy is a scumbag, I need some advice on how to get rid of this dirt ball, and look innocent, sure as hell not how I tried to rid myself of my first husband."

Dick fell over in a drunken stupor snoring loudly.

Brenda slowly slid out of bed grabbing a pillow, and headed for the couch. She woke up at six thirty in the morning, and quickly dressed, if she told her father he would shoot the son of a bitch. Her best bet was to have a talk with her uncle who she knew would keep a cool head, and would know how to seek retribution. Her daughter had stayed overnight with a friend so she was safe from Dick, who was sleeping off his drunk. Brenda started her car, and pulled out of the driveway as slowly as possible, making sure not to wake him, as soon as the car was on the blacktop she pushed the petal to the metal. Pulling in front of her uncles office at eight fifteen, sometimes he would sleep in the office, hoping that would be the case today. She parked the car, shut off the ignition, opening the car door it gave a loud creak."The noise is driving me nuts,I have to get it fixed."

Walking to the upstairs entrance, rang the bell waited about thirty seconds, and rang again this time she kept her finger on the bell. As the ringing sound floated down the stairs there was a loud thump, and the intercom came alive.

"Who the hell is ringing the bell? It's only eight o'clock in the morning, you crazy bastard."

"Uncle Frank, this is Brenda, she answered," I need some advice like now.""Brenda, get your skinny little ass up here, and tell your Uncle Frank your troubles."

She heard the buzzer, and opened the door. Brenda bounded up the stairs , opened the office door and flung her herself on Uncle Frank, and started to cry,"I have a horrible problem."She broke down and started to cry uncontrollably, sobbing with tears streaming down her cheeks, all the while talking deep breaths as if she would suffocate. Her Uncle Frank became very concerned,"What in the hell is going on?"

Brenda sat in the chair that faced his desk, then walked around and sat facing her. She started,"If my dad knew what was going on he would kill the fucking pervert","Wow, Wow, slow down, tell me from the beginning."her Uncle cautions.

Brenda tells the story how she met Dick, and that they have been living together for six months, and how he has become very abusive,"He has threatened to kill me and my daughter if I mention anything about his sexual abuse, it is getting worse every day."He sat quietly thinking this sure fits the portfolio I have on this weirdo, but he couldn't let Brenda know this. She rambles on,"To spite my parents, I shacked up with this guy because my father had his nose in my business, and I was pissed because he knew my ex was screwing every woman that opened her legs and wanted a strange piece of cock."

Frank puts his hand on her shoulder and says,"Calm down, calm down, so far this putz has not caused any real physical damage, but it sure sounds like it could be his next move. Brenda how far do you want to go with this, do you want to put him away for a few years, never to lay his eyes on you or yours again?"Brenda sobs."Yes absolutely, he is a psychopath, and without control he is going to hurt me or worse my daughter."

Her Uncle Frank wrote a few things on a piece of paper, and when he was finished, they put their heads together and as they talked a plan began to form. Her uncle reminded her.

"Remember what we discussed tonight, you have to follow it to the letter, just as we planned, do you understand?" Brenda shook her head yes, with tears in here yes.

CHAPTER TEN

BRINGING DOWN THE HAMMER

The locker room on the Dredge was a little hole in the wall with just enough room for six lockers, and a bench to sit on while changing clothes Dick had just gotten out of the shower, and was toweling off, it was eight thirty in the evening.

He had worked a twelve hour shift, the powers to be had approved the overtime the channel used for navigation was to be deeper than previously planned, and the amount of sludge and dirt to be removed from the river channel would extend the job an extra month, this backed up the dredges, and barges for quite awhile.

Dick had been staying clear of Olof and Sammy since dumping the gun in the river. He felt it was used to keep his mouth shut, and implicate him in case he had thought about going to the police. That creepy feeling running down his spine was still there ever since Olof had joined the crew something wasn't right.

Sammy walked into the locker room and asked,"Dick why don't you come and have a drink with me and Olof after work?"Dick begged off,"I'll have one drink, but then I have to screw,I have a heavy date with my squeeze, so I'll have just one and take my leave. Sorry about that."

Dick was afraid Sammy was going to knock over another gas station when we pulled the last heist Sammy pistol whipped the attendant, it made him totally gun shy. He thought,"What if that crazy fuck killed someone for a few bucks that was nuts, it's as if I don't have enough problems with out worrying about that shit."

Besides, he wanted to get home and knock off another piece. Brenda had been pretty docile as of late, she did as she was told when they were in bed together. The better for her, it would take more time to break her in, but she had come around to see who ran the house, including the sex scene, as long as she behaved he wouldn't have to beat her ass.

The FBI had received an anonymous letter about six months prior, concerning drugs coming into Philadelphia. It had been six months since Olof had joined the crew, there was still the weekly pickup, Olof took his payoff, and helped Sammy and the first mate handle the goods keeping his mouth closed. Things remained the same. Sammy and the First Mate still appeared to be the main conspirators, as usual the rest of the crew just went along, and kept their mouths shut, and the captain was nowhere to be found. Olof reported once a week to the Pennsylvania State Police and the FBI, they had a tail on the First Mate, Sammy and Dick, after the first month Dick was ruled out of the equation, Dick helped with the drugs like the rest of the crew, but didn't seem to have anything to do with distribution of the drugs. Like the rest of the crew it couldn't be proven that they had any knowledge of what was being picked up.

The First Mate and Sammy were the only ones that made the drops or took the merchandise to shore and distributed it in the city. This evening Sammy and Olof were gearing to knock over a store, and Sammy was carrying the drugs so he could make a drop downtown then they could take down a Convenience Store.

All this was unbeknown to Dick whose sense of preservation was right on track. The FBI had accumulated enough evidence to arrest all the players involved they had traced the drops and pickups to the Philly mob, Sammy was their main target, he would be allowed to make the drop arrest him after the fact, and see if they could turn him, and use him as a Federal Witness. Everything was in place. The Coast Guard was alerted to stop the tramp steamer suspected of carrying the drugs, board her, silence the radio, make sure the crew was put out of action, the FBI had traced the registry to Panama.

The State Police and FBI had a three pronged attack, stop the tramp steamer, raid the dredge, and follow Sammy, and Olof to the drop. It all had to happen in one fell swoop or the perpetrators would have a chance to dump the evidence and disappear.

Dick had showered and changed into his civilian clothes, when Sammy and Olof walked into the shower room Sammy waved to him. Dick looked up saying, "I'll meet you guys at our local hangout, like I said one and done I have a date."

He left the dredge, and climbed into his car, he had been driving alone for the last couple of weeks and swore the Dredge was under surveillance, there always seemed to be a truck parked along the road approaching the dredge, no matter where they were working there was a car or truck sitting, and lately motor boats were cruising the waterway.

He drove to the local bar, and noticed a State Store across the street,"I'll pick up the fifth of liquor when I leave the bar." He entered the bar and called to the barkeep,"Sal how have you been?"

The bartender mumbled something under his breath,"This guy is a schmuck, OK what do you need?"Dick orders,"Give me a draft and a shot of CC."The bartender poured the draft set it on the bar, filled a shot glass with the CC,"That will be ninety five cents."Dick laid down a dollar,"keep the change."About twenty minutes later Sammy and Olof walked in. Dick could tell Sammy was zipped up on something, looking at Sammy, Dick knew he was getting ready to pull a stickup. Sammy ordered a double bourbon and a draft, he waited for the bartender to pour a double shot and place the draft beer on the bar, Sammy took a drink from the draft beer, picked up the double bourbon, and poured it in the beer making a joke,"Nothing like a boilermaker, best drink in town."

He was holding a couple of pills, threw his head back popped the pills into his mouth took a big swig of his boilermaker, with this he roared,"this is going to be one hell of a night, some sucker is going to pay big time." Olof just looked at Sammy slapping him on the back and replied,"You sure got that right, bartender give me a draft."Dick drank his shot, and beer and headed for the door, Sammy hollered,"where in the hell are you going?" He looked back and answered as he went through the door,"home to see my squeeze."

He kept on going, he knew if he hesitated he would never get out of the bar, Sammy was really getting cocked, he had that killer look in his eye, and his body language spelled Danger, Danger!!

After Dick left Sammy ordered another Boilermaker, Olof tried to get him to leave he wanted to target the drop, and wrap it up, but Sammy would have none of it he ordered a third Boilermaker and Olof said to Sammy,"I thought we had a few places to go tonight?, we'll never get there at this rate, weren't you supposed to make a meet at ten twenty? it's ten now we better get moving."

This got Sammy's attention,"Yea, they will be pissed if I'm late, let's get the hell out of here, hey barkeep give me a chit on that last drink,OK?,we have to leave." Sammy walked to the door turned to Olof,"Lets get this drop over with, and then we can have some fun."

Olof breathed a sigh of relief,"at last I, thought this wacko was going to blow the stakeout." Sammy was driving a brand new Cadillac, Olof wondered how in the hell he could afford a new caddy, he had to be with the mob. They climbed into the Caddy, nice leather interior, custom dashboard, and all the latest gadgets, the ride to the drop was fifteen minutes, Sammy pulled up to an abandoned warehouse, and blinked the car lights three times, out of the shadows pulls a Ford Pickup the lights turned off, drives around to the Caddy's trunk and stops. Sammy gets out of the car, walks to the rear and pops the trunk. Olof viewing this through the rear view mirror sees this ape jump down from the truck, he was as big, as the truck door. About six feet and went at least three hundred pounds, had a face only a mother could love, meanwhile out of the passenger door steps his twin brother he mutters,"A hell of a welcoming committee."

Sammy hands out two packages, closes the trunk walked back to the car, starts it and drives away not looking back. The police have eyes on the drop, and were given orders to follow the pickup truck, but under no circumstances to move in, just observe.

Sammy starts laughing like a crazy man, pulls out a bottle of pills and pops two more, he yells,"Yea, ha, we'll go have some fun."Olof had no idea what this crazy high fuck was up to now. Sammy said,"Let's get some gas,I know a gas station that's open till midnight.

Olof looked at the gas gauge the tank was full he thinks,"I remember reading in the reports, that Sammy was suspected of robbing gas stations. This asshole is going to rob this station, I'll let him go in first, and pop him."Sammy pulls up to the gas pump, jumps out of the Caddy, and heads straight for the door. Olof jumped out reaching for his black jack his only thought is,"I have to stop him before he kills somebody."

Sammy pushes the door open with a bang and yells,"Put your hands up, and empty the register, or I will blow your head off."He raised his pistol to shoot the clerk, there was a loud click and that was the last thing

Sammy remembered. Olof called in the robbery after he sapped Sammy. Olof"That blackjack sure came in handy", he made the store clerk sit down and decompress, when the police arrived he knew not to move and keep his gun

out of sight. The Philly cops were known to be trigger happy, Olof had notified the FBI and State Police to let them know about the latest incident he asked,"How do you want me to proceed from here?"

He was ordered by the FBI to cuff him, and bring Sammy in this would be a perfect time to turn him and when the Philadelphia Police arrived, tell them to call the station and forget everything they saw. The problem had been taken care of."Olof hoped to keep this quiet for a couple of hours, the strike team wasn't due to raid the dredge till midnight, the squad car pulled up with sirens blaring, the officers dismounted their guns drawn, Olof waited for them to enter the Gas Station, he stood there holding his badge,"I am an undercover officer, the FBI will be here in a few minutes you are to stand down."

As he spoke the FBI pulled in and parked, the two agents disembarked from their car, on entering the store they immediately told the officers,"we will take over from here, you will keep radio silence, the precinct has been alerted, so back down immediately."The local police gave the FBI some blow back,"Who in the hell do you suits think you are, this is our bust why don't you butt out?" Agent Williams walks to the officers and gives them an order,"You were told to stand down, there is more going on than meets the eye , gentlemen holster your weapons, and please go sit in your cruiser."

The Philadelphia Police holstered their weapons, and walked out of the store returning to their Police car.

Agent Williams looked at Olof whispering,"lets get this stupid ass out of here, cuff him, and frisk him for any hidden weapons."Williams looks at the clerk and putting a finger to his lips says,"Yea, I mean you, keep your mouth shut this goes no further this never happened if you open your trap I will charge you with disobeying a federal officer."The clerk just stood there shaking his head up and down to show he understood.

Williams gave Olof his orders,"Help me put Sammy in my car, you drive his Caddy and follow me we will store it a tour facility, I recommend you return to your post your cover has been blown, we strike in less than an hour, and cannot afford any slip ups."When they arrived at FBI headquarters, Sammy was put in a holding cell Olof was given a car and told to return to his Barracks.

Sammy was awake, but still groggy, he had no idea how he ended up in a cell, all he remembered was walking into the store, and now here he was in a holding cell, being questioned by the FBI. The Agents had chained his feet to the floor, the steel table he was sitting at was bolted to the concrete floor, and his wrists cuffed to a steel bar on the table. He looked around and thought,"These fucks have me dead to rights I'm so tied up I can't even scratch my balls."

Agent Williams walked into the Interrogation Room with a smile on his face he leaned over the table and started the questioning"Sammy, Sammy, Sammy, I have waited along time to catch your ass, we have had our eyes on you forever. Let me give you a little update, running drugs, robbery and who knows what else, if we keep digging maybe murder, all we need from you is who controls the drug trade. We need the distributors and I will make sure you receive a very lenient sentence."He just gave a grunt, and laughed,"what do you think I am nuts? if I go to prison I will be dead in a week you Feds go screw." Without a word Agent Williams stood up, flexed a phone book two or three times, gave it to the Agent next to him and as he exited the the Interrogation Room said,"You know what to do, and don't be gentle."

Sammy looked up and glanced at Agent Woys holding the phone book. Agent Woys was six four, close cropped black hair with a hint of gray at the temples, a nineteen inch neck, fifty inch chest, dark brown eyes, and a rock solid jaw. He had served five years in the Airborne Rangers had the rank of Captain, his time on the front lines in Korea had steeled his personality. His unit was half One Hundred and First Airborne and the other half was a South Korean Tiger Unit they would drop behind enemy lines and harass the the Chinese. The entire contingent prided themselves fighting with cold steel when the Chinese encountered the the battalion they literally shit in their pants. When anyone in the unit drew a bayonet or a knife, before it could be sheathed the weapon had to draw the enemies blood, or their own before they could stand down. In other words Agent Woys was not a man to be screwed with.

Standing in the Interrogation Room, Woys walked around the table, and banged Sammy's head twice with the phone book hollering,"Come on you stupid son of a bitch, give me the names of the distributors or I will beat your head to mush."Sammy let out a groan,"What the hell, you are one crazy son of a mother I don't know-anything."

Agent Woys whacked Sammy's head three more times, and retired to a corner in the Interrogation Room. A second Agent sat down in front of Sammy and started a dialogue,"Look, we don't really want to do this, just give us the names and you can go free. The other agent looked at Woys and asked him,"Can you get us a couple cups of coffee, and some donuts?, Sammy looks as if he needs something to perk him up."Woys gives Sammy a dirty look and exits the room.

Meanwhile the FBI, State Police, and Coast Guard have set their plan into motion, exactly at midnight the Coast Guard has stopped and boarded the Tramp Steamer that was carrying the drugs, shut down their radio, and corralled the twelve man crew they had no way to communicate with the dredge or anyone on the outside, another Coast Guard cutter with six FBI agents armed with machine guns and tear gas pulled alongside the dredge.

State Police cordoned off the docks, and blocked traffic from entering and leaving the area, after boarding the dredge the First Mate was immediately cuffed, the rest of the crew stood with their hands up, the Agents banged on the Captains door, as usual he wasn't on deck when the boarding took place they banged on the door a second time calling,"Open the door this is the FBI, I said open the door."A voice answered from the Captain's quarters,"The door is unlocked."The Agents kicked the door open, their guns ready, behind the desk sat the Captain, studying navigation charts, the Captain looks up saying,"Gentlemen can I help you?"Answering in unison,"Who in the hell do you think you are?, we just raided your dredge and confiscated the drugs."The Captain was absolutely non- pulsed, he motioned to the Agents to look at something on his desk, as they looked down the Captain flips over a paper on his desk and lo and behold there was an FBI badge. The Captain shrugged his shoulders.

"I guess you have to cuff me, and arrest me with the rest of the crew, or J. Edgar Hoover will be very upset."

CHAPTER ELEVEN

THE BEGINNING OF THE END

Dick walked to the State Store, and bought a fifth of bourbon. He stood in the State Store's doorway to see if Sammy and Olof had left, the Caddy was still parked in front of his car."What the hell", he thought," let me get the frigging out of here before Sammy corrals me into doing something stupid."Dick walked the half a block back to his car, started the engine, and drove away from the bar. When he pulled into the driveway of the house he could see that Brenda and her daughter were home. "Let me cool it till later tonight", he thought. He shut the engine off, grabbed the fifth of bourbon, and walked up the sidewalk to the house. When he stepped into the living room, Brenda and Sara were sitting at the kitchen table, she was helping her daughter with her homework.

Dick gave a short,"Hi!"Walked to the nearest lounge chair plopped down and hollered,"Sara, bring me a glass of ice."Sara answered before Brenda could stop her,I'm not your servant get it yourself."Brenda immediately scolds Sara,"Don't be a smart ass, get Dick a glass with ice now, and I mean it."Dick hollered back,"Look you little bitch, I will break you like I did your mother now bring me a glass and some ice."

Brenda looked at Sara, and motioned with her hand."Get the glass, and some ice, and keep your mouth shut."Sara did as she was told. Dick opened the bourbon, and poured it over the ice till the glass was full. He sat back on the couch took a drink thinking."I'll make that bitch pay ten fold, I never took any lip from my ex-wife, son or daughter, and I sure as hell won't take any guff in this house."

Brenda is sitting in the kitchen watching Dick. "Sure hope he drinks himself into a stupor, and falls asleep on the couch, I don't need that slug next to me tonight."She waited till Dick fell asleep on the couch and said."Sara."Get your jammies on, and we can snuggle in your bed, Dick is drunk on the couch, so we should be safe.""AW mom, that sounds creepy. Do I have to?",Sara answers."You just do as I ask, please Sara work with me, OK!"Sara agreed still feeling something was not quite right. Brenda waited for Sara to get into her pajamas, and they crawled into bed, and quickly fell asleep. The hall clock chimed it was two am, Dick rolled over, almost falling off the couch, his head was throbbing he sat up thinking," Where in the hell is everyone, I wonder what the frack time it is? I need a drink, my mouth tastes like a cat shit in it."He stumbles into the kitchen opens, the refrigerator, and spies a pitcher of lemonade picks it up, and pours the liquid into his mouth. He drinks with such gusto that most of the lemonade misses his mouth, flows down his chin, soaks his shirt and leaves a gooey puddle that encircles his feet in a sticky mess on the kitchen floor placing the pitcher back in the refrigerator, he grabs the shirt,Dick talking to himself.

"Jesus Christ, Dick you are a real slob I better change before I get into bed."He drops the shirt on the kitchen floor, and uses it to mop up the spilled lemonade. After pushing it around a few times with his left foot, looks down at the mess and thought."Screw this I'll let Brenda clean it up tomorrow, that's what women are for, cleaning up."He stumbles out of the kitchen, and into the master bedroom.

"What the hell, where is Brenda? That bitch must be sleeping in her daughters bedroom, I'm going to yank her ass out of there."But before he could do the deed he falls face first into the bed, still shirtless, his pants around his ankles, smelling like booze, and falls into a deep coma like sleep. At six am the alarm went off,Brenda rolled over looking at the clock, it was time to rise and shine. Her shift started at eight touching Sara's shoulder shook her gently."Come on baby it's time to get up, I'll take you to school. You can wait in study hall till school starts."

Sara rolled over, and started to reply, her mother put her finger to her lips."Let's keep it quiet, we don't want to wake Dick I'm sure he will be in a bad mood, and have a roaring hangover. So let's not disturb him, OK?" Sara just shook her head yes, rolled out of bed putting her feet on the floor, standing up, shaking herself awake, her mother looking at Sara thinking," she was growing up too fast."

After they were dressed Brenda and Sara tiptoed down the hall past the bedroom where Dick was sleeping. She wanted to grab some breakfast with Sara, and then drop her off at school. Dick never woke up so she was smiling when they entered the diner, finally having pulled one over on him.

Brenda had to start implementing the plan her and Uncle Frank had talked about. No matter how she felt it was the only way to break free,

Dick was continually threatening to kill everyone in her family if she opened her mouth about his sexual encounters, Brenda had no doubt the crazy bastard would do it, Brenda thought," Tonight I will lay the ground work to get that scum out of my life permanently."

CHAPTER TWELVE

THE SNITCH

Sammy was still in the holding room he had not been released from his chair to go to the bathroom for two days, he was not given any utensils when he ate, the Agents only released his left hand, so he had to scoop up the food to feed himself. Agent Woys was a master at breaking down the physical, and mental barriers of any prisoner no matter how strong they appeared to be.

He was chafing with shit in his pants, he had urinated down his legs at least a half a dozen times. The door opened, and Agent Woys entered with a phone book in his hand. Sammy groaned."Holy Christ, please let me cleanup."

Woys had plugged his nose with Vicks to keep out the stench, and was wearing a surgical mask. He had learned this little trick when he came in contact with a rotting enemy corpses. He was definitely on the verge of breaking, Sammy had tears running down his cheeks, and sobbing all at the same time. Agent Woys had a smirk on his face as he walked over to Sammy, and raised the phone book to strike him on the back of the head,"I'll tell you everything I know, Please don't hit me again, my head is splitting, I can't see straight."he bleated out. Agent Woys just smiled laid the phone book on the table in front of Sammy,"It's here just in case you are bull shitting me."

Sammy pleaded,"At least let me shower, and put on some clean clothes."Woys snickered and handed Sammy a pad and pencil."You start writing, and when you finish I will let you shower and change clothes if you screw with me, you'll be dressed in your shitty clothes, and we will start all over again, and this time I won't be so nice."

Sammy at that point had broken down completely, he sobbed. "Anything, anything you want."

Woys pointed to the pad and pencil,"Now write who the people are who run the organization, when you finish I'll let you shower and give you a change of clothes, then we can get into the meat of how the organization works."

He walks to the door, and raps on it three times, and calls to the other Agents,"Open up, and get our friend some clean clothes, let him shower as long as he likes, bring in the leg irons, and manacles make sure he keeps them on while he showers."

Two Agents walk into the room, one of the Agents un- cuffs his hands, then the leg irons, he had been sitting so long he had to be helped to stand upright, he was told. "Strip off your clothes, and leave them on the floor, then hold out your hands so we can put on the manacles."He was wrapped in a large beach towel, and led out of the Interrogation Room to the showers. Sammy felt like he was in heaven the hot water running over his body felt better than sex, scrubbing himself at least six times trying to remove the stink from his skin. The guards had been given specific orders, at no time were they to take their eyes off of the prisoner in case he attempted suicide or tried to escape.

Sammy had only one idea, clean the stink off, and see what kind of deal he could cut without going to jail.

CHAPTER THIRTEEN

NIGHTY,NIGHT

Around nine o'clock Brenda called to her daughter,"Come to bed with mother."Sara hollers back,"I will not, sounds nasty."Brenda called softly,"Baby put your nighty on, and please come to bed with mother, you can sleep on the edge of the bed,""Aw mom, that sounds gross."

"Get your butt in here, and crawl under the covers now!!" Sara stomps her foot, and then walks into the bedroom,

her mother says soothingly," Now climb under the covers, and just snuggle down, Dick is in the parlor so don't worry we'll be sound asleep by the time he comes in."

Meanwhile Dick was doing his evening imbibing. He had heard about the raid on the dredge, and was trying to figure out if he was in deep enough to get his ass arrested. Sammy had dropped out of sight, nobody seemed to know where he was, as long as Sammy was incognito he was safe. Dick poured himself another glass of whiskey, holding up the bottle to see how much was left, the bottle was half full, he sets the whiskey carefully on the table thinking."I've had enough for tonight I need a piece of tail, and when I get drunk I can't even get it up",Dick turned one hundred eighty degrees, faced the hall and walked toward the bedroom with only one thought in mind. He stopped momentarily at the bedroom door, turned the knob with force as he entered stopping in his tracks,"What the frack is this, what is she doing in our bed?"

Brenda put her hand over Sara's mouth answering,"She was scared, and could not sleep."Dick was furious,"Get her out of this fucking bed."Brenda rolled over looking at Dick," I'll take care of you, why don't we go into the bathroom."

While they were in the bathroom Sara had fallen asleep, the next thing she knew her mother was shaking her," Wake up baby, it's time for school."

Brenda, Dick, and Sara went through the week normally.

Saturday night she coaxed her daughter into bed, only this time she had her daughter sleep in the middle. Dick came home half flagged, having stopped off at the neighborhood bar, and trying to pick up a couple of locals who bushed him off."Dick go home to your mommy, we're not interested."

He stumbled out of the bar mumbling to himself," God damned women they are all a pain in my ass, that goes for my first wife and the one I'm living with."He had a very short span when it came to women, his mother came, and went her entire life, he never had a chance to grow close to her or his two sisters, who were wild children in their own right. At an early age his father had abandoned the family, and disappeared never to be heard from again. "Screw this I'm going home to get a piece of ass."

Dick climbed into his car, it was a fifteen minute drive to the house, pulling into the driveway, noticed the house lights were out he looked at his watch was one thirty in the morning. He felt in his pocket looking for his keys, put them in his hand, and staggered toward the house.

The light over the front door had been left on so he had no trouble finding the lock, Dick barged in like the drunken boor he was, he could care less if he woke everyone up, and headed straight to the bedroom.

The bedroom door swings open, and he looks, then takes a second look, what is going on, there are two people in the bed mother, and daughter maybe we can have a "m'enage a' trois", without hesitation he stripped off his clothes, and pulls back the covers. Brenda seeing Dick rolls over.

Sara was dead asleep, she allows him to mount her, she moans, and groans to keep his attention till he came, and rolled over dead asleep,"What was that mommy?"Sara asks half asleep."It's OK honey, just go back to sleep."her mother answers.

At six am Brenda was awake as usual, jumped out of bed, and readied for her waitress job. She tucked the blanket around her daughter, kissed her on the forehead, and whispered,"I love you."

As she wiped a tear from her cheek, walked out of the bedroom, and didn't stop till she was in her car heading to the diner. Dick looked up, and saw Sara,"Well, well what have we hear?"

He had a thing for young girls, knowing how to manipulate them sexually, but never taking their virginity. He knew where to touch, and kiss to screw up their minds, making little girls unsure of themselves, so that he could have his way. He rolled over, and did as he wished.

Brenda's shift was over at two in the afternoon, she had been thinking about Sara all day as soon as she arrived home, when she entered the house, she called Sara's name very quietly."Sara, Sara, honey are you home?"Walking into the kitchen she spotted a note on the table,"Mom went to visit my girlfriend down the street, Sara."

Dick walked into the kitchen wearing only his shorts, Brenda looked at him trying to read his body language thinking."Had anything happened between Dick, and her daughter?"He was in a good mood,"Good morning, how was your day at work? I made a pot of coffee it's on the stove, do you want a cup?"

Brenda was taken aback,"What in the hell was going on?"It seemed her plan was backfiring, just then Sara walked into the house all smiles,"Hi mom, how was your day?"

She walked over to her mother, and gave her a kiss on the cheek. At that moment Dick exited the bathroom, only this time he was dressed. Sara looked his way, and said,"You look pretty sharp, you going out?"

Brenda almost lost her teeth Sara hated Dick, and was always looking to start a fight with him it could have been her imagination, but she sensed a bond between them, she wanted to freak out, but held her cool. Inside she was shaking, and felt as if she would throw up, "I have to see Uncle Frank."she thought,"This entire plan seems to be getting out of hand."

Brenda tells Dick, and Sara,"will be back in an hour, have to pick up groceries."

With that she turned abruptly, and walked to her car, when she was comfortably in her car, she started to hyperventilate, she was having trouble breathing she felt sure as hell that she was going to pass out. After four or five minutes she was breathing normal. Started the car, and as she was backing out of the driveway starting to shake again,"Fuck, what in the hell is wrong with me?"

Brenda knew in the back of her mind what the problem was, but didn't want to admit it,"This plan has turned to shit, shit!"When Brenda had stopped shaking, pulled into the street, and drove to her Uncle Franks office. The trip took about twenty minutes to drive to his office, there was a parking space near the office she parked, shut off the engine, pulled out the keys, was out of the car in a flash, and is banging on her Uncles door in a fury, ringing the bell, she held the bell down till it hurt she was thinking,"you better be in Uncle, we have a major problem."

Frank watched Brenda when she pulled to the curb, he could tell by her body language there was trouble brewing, when she reached the office door she was pushing the buzzer, he was reciprocating she swung the door open, and Frank could hear Brenda taking the stairs two at a time, her Uncle moved to open the door before Brenda reached it.

She literally ran into his office, she was breathless, tears streaming down her cheeks, Uncle Frank,"What's the matter?, sit down, relax and take a deep breath, tell me what is going on."

He poured her a stiff glass of bourbon, she picked up the glass with both hands, they were shaking so bad. She blurted out,"that bastard has seduced my daughter." Frank sat back in his chair, not believing what he just heard."Brenda are you sure, have you actually seen or heard anything? "No, but until this morning Sara hated his guts, now the two of them are good friends. I almost puked I had to leave the house before I went nuts."

Frank thinks,"We have to set things up"ASAP"before they turn real nasty, when this goes down I want you no where to be found, you cannot be tied to this or you will be complicit. "Brenda do you understand what I am saying?"She just nodded her head, yes. Frank repeats,"Do you understand?"

Keep them apart till next Saturday set it up for early morning, when you leave make sure the front and back doors are unlocked I will call Sergeant Jones, and tell him Dick is ready to be taken down, and set up the raid on the house hopefully the police will catch them in bed together."Brenda starts sobbing, and wringing her hands,

"Oh god is this the only way to rid myself of him?" "Now calm down, this creep is not known for penetration, that's the only thing has kept him out of jail your father warned you about this asshole, and you ignored him."

She started to sob uncontrollably , her Uncle gave her an unforgiving look."Pull your shit together, and let's get this over with before it gets out of hand is there a phone nearby at a neighbors house, or how about a phone booth? I will set it up with the local precinct Now get your skinny butt to work, and do exactly as we discussed."

Brenda wiped the tears from her eyes, stood up, and without any comment walked out of the office her legs sagged, and she staggered down the office stairs shaking like a leaf. Her Uncle was right, this had to be completed Saturday as planned. When she left, Frank picked up the phone, and called his friend at the station.

Sergeant Jones picked up the phone on the second ring,"

Hello, Sergeant Jones here."Frank made the message short, and sweet,"The scene has been set for early Saturday morning. How fast can you move on the target?"

Sergeant Jones replied,"When I get the call I will be able to respond in less than twenty minutes, he has been on my radar for quite awhile."

He placed the phone in it's cradle, he had a strange look of satisfaction thinking."This prick is going to be taken down hard, real hard."

Brenda made sure Sara stayed at her girlfriends, or her parents house all week, on Saturday she was allowed to return to the house. The week had seemed to drag on forever. Saturday evening Brenda called to her daughter, "Sara honey, come to bed with mother."

Sara without answering came romping into the bedroom, she was dressed in a little pink teddy. Her mother gave her a slight admonishment."Why in the hell are you dressed like that for bed? ,especially since Dick will be here in a couple of minutes."Brenda asked.

Sara answered,"I'll be under the covers, he won't see anything. Mother and daughter were snuggled under the covers, drifting off to sleep when Dick walked into the bedroom wearing only his briefs looking long, and hard at the sleeping forms in the bed."Well, well tonight will be lots of fun."He climbed into bed, and thought as he fell asleep,"Four O'clock sounds like a good time for donkey dipping." Brenda woke at three in the am, quietly slid out of bed, walked to the window, and deliberately parted the curtains ever so slightly walked to the bathroom and put on her makeup, got dressed, tip toed to the rear of the house and opened the bolt on the screen door. She unlatched the inner door and left a note,"I am starting work early", on the kitchen table.

When she left the house the front door was left ajar.

Instead of leaving immediately she walked around to the side of the house, peeking into the bedroom.

Dick had rolled over, and was next to her daughter, she watched as Dick pulled back the covers, and started to caress her back. Brenda broke her stare, and quietly stole away from the house, when she came to the corner of the house, took off running to the corner pay phone, dropped in a dime, and called her Uncle, he picked up immediately all she said was,"now is the time,"and hung up.

Frank called Sergeant Jones, who was two blocks away waiting for the call on the Police radio, he signaled the two police cars to converge on the residence."Lets not screw this up, I need a car at the back door, and a car in front, the photographer will lead the assault, the doors are unlocked, now let's get the bastard."

The Police were in place in less than five minutes, the team slowly opened the back, and front doors simultaneously, the bedroom door was pushed open, as the photographer raised his camera, Dick was in the process of removing Sara's underpants. He was naked,"what the fuck is this",he hollered. All of a sudden before Dick or Sara knew what was happening, there was a bright flash, and another bright flash. They were both blinded, Sara was naked from the waist down, and Dick was totally nude the Police threw Dick on the other side of the bed, and cuffed him. A female Social Worker grabbed Sara, and practically dragged her to her own bedroom where she was taken into State custody.

Dick was dragged out of the house still naked, one of the cops grabbed a blanket, and wrapped it around him as he was placed into the Police car Dick and Sara were still in a daze trying to understand what in the hell had just happened. Sara was placed in protective custody Dick was fingerprinted, had his picture taken, and placed in a cell under suicide watch. Sara was placed in an interrogation room, and let sit by herself after an hour the door opened, and the Social Worker entered followed by a plain clothes Detective, they both sat down facing her, and the Social Worker broke the silence."How are you doing Sara, do you understand what this is all about?" Sara began to cry, she sniffed,"What did I do wrong?" "You are thirteen, under age, and apparently having sexual encounters with your mothers boyfriend."Sara answered,"Dick said it was OK, because it felt good and not to tell my mother."The Social Worker sat back and questioned Sara,"so your mother didn't know anything about your sexual contact with him?"Sara shook her head answering,"No, when we were playing, my mom was at work."

Frank waited for an hour before he called Brenda to let her know that the Police had succeeded in catching Sara, and Dick in the act he guaranteed Dick would be put away for a long, long time. Brenda broke down at work, and began to cry, she had to see her daughter. All this was necessary to get that pig out of her life.

The Police let Dick sit in his cell till noon, a guard banged on the bars and hollered,"hey asshole put your hands through the slot in the bars so I can cuff you." He rolled off the bunk, and walked to the prison bars, and put his hands through the door slot. The guard clicked on the cuffs, and opened the cell door,"let's go Dickey boy, Sergeant Jones wants to have a talk with you."

Dick just "grunted" and was led to the interrogation room, he was told to sit down, and the guard left the room, closing the door with a bang that made Dick jump. He was still in a fog."What the hell is happening."

Sergeant Jones entered the Interrogation Room, and sat down facing Dick,"well, well Dick we have your ass nailed to the wall."

He laid a dozen pictures on the table in front of him, Dick looked, and looked, there he was doing the deed,and there was Sara naked from the waist down. He could feel his gonads shrivel up as he gazed at the pictures,before he could utter a word Sergeant Jones said"I have you asshole. If you don't want to go away for a minimum of five to ten, just sign the confession, and you will get three to five. Oh, by the way your buddy Sammy gave you up on the Gas Station robbery, so we can add on another ten."

Of course that was bull shit, Sammy had ratted on the Copos, but had never mentioned the robberies for fear of getting in deeper. Sergeant Jones could tell he had hit a nerve, Dick turned white as the blood drained out of his face. He started to speak, but all that came out was,"How in the hell did all this shit come down?"

Sergeant Jones just smiled,"You fucking pervert, you conned your way out of two other situations with young girls, not counting the robberies this time we have you dead to rights, now sign the confession, and save me a lot of time in court, because I will crucify you, I have had my eyes on you for a long time."Dick started to shake, and tears started to run down his cheeks, and as he was shaking blurted out,"I need a lawyer."

Sergeant Jones was getting frustrated,"You keep me in court I will fry you. I talked to the parents of both girls you molested, and they will gladly reopen their cases, and refile charges against you. If you don't take the three to five I will charge you with three felonies, and you will go up for life."His hands were still shaking as he reached across the table, pulled over the confession, and signed it. Sergeant Jones just smiled, his bluff had worked, he had interviewed both sets of parents concerning the sexual assaults.

Their answer was,"No way would they let themselves, and their daughters get mixed up in that mess again, as far as they were concerned it was in the past."

When the guard arrived to return him to his cell his legs were shaking so hard he needed help standing up his court date was set three weeks hence. As he couldn't make bail, he would be sitting in a cell until his court date.

Three weeks went by, and early in the morning of the trial the guard banged on bars."Lets go brother, time to rise and shine, you need to shower, and shave, and by the way your sister brought you clean clothes for the trial."

After he cleaned up, he was shackled, and placed in a police van. He was driven to the court house, ushered into an elevator, and when they reached the first floor he was escorted into a small conference room his legal consul was waiting for him."Dick, you have already signed a confession, do you want to change your plea, or have me try to get you a jury trial?, I have to know right now, before we enter the court room.""No, I copped a plea,let it stand as is."Dick retorted.

His consul had been prepped before hand, he was told there would be no jury trial, only a judge and a couple of witnesses, and after the recess the Judge would pass sentence, Dick was led into the courtroom and told to be seated. The first witness called was Brenda the District Attorney asked her a few questions concerning Dicks threatening to kill her family, and she was shown the pictures taken by the Police photographer. Brenda broke down and cried, swore she had no knowledge of Dick's prior sexual conduct, and was allowed to leave the jury box. The second witness was Sara, she was asked if he was present in the court room."Yes, that is Dick sitting in the front row."Sara then started to shake, and the Judge dismissed her. Dick had an epiphany, this entire thing was a setup, the bitch had sacrificed her daughter to get rid of him, he attempted to jump out of the chair, but was restrained by two court marshals. The Judge brought down his gavel.

"If you attempt that again, I will have you restrained and gagged, do you understand that kind of conduct will not be tolerated in my court room."He looked at the Judge, then his Lawyer, and knew he was screwed this was a kangaroo court, his fate was sealed. The last witness was Sergeant Jones. His testimony sealed the case, there was no doubt what had transpired between Dick, and Sara. The Judge called a recess after an hour the Judge re- entered the courtroom and asked Dick how he pleaded,he hesitated, his lawyer leaned over and whispered."Answer yes, or you will get another five years."

"Guilty your honor."

The Judge spoke to the court before passing sentence. "The prisoner should have received a sentence of five to ten years, but because he has confessed, and saved the state time, and money, the sentence will be three to five on condition that he never speaks to Brenda, Sara or any of her family, approach to within one thousand feet. He cannot call or threaten her family in any manner or any family or friends involved in this case should you do so I will put you away for another five years. Do you understand?"

Dick looked at the Judge answering,"Yes your honor." So here he was having to serve three to five years. "That bitch set me up, and if I even look at her sideways they will put me away for another five. This cunt has a screw loose."

The Judge then remanded Sara over to the Social workers, she was to be rehabilitated, and held in child care for at least six months. Dick was taken back to his cell. The next morning he was given prison stripes, and transported to the big house. Dick was a big man in his own right,and there was no way in hell he was going to let someone use him as their bitch. Dick knew a few of the boys in the slammer, so he immediately became one of the boys.

After a couple of years of good behavior, he was paroled from prison, his clothes no longer fit, having spent every day in prison lifting weights to deter any of his fellow prisoners from getting any ideas.

Dick boarded a bus for for center city, his sister had rented a small apartment, and set him up with a part time job. His ex- wife, and children wouldn't have anything to do with him, while in prison he had only thought"Revenge" every night he fantasized how he would maim her, and her fucking daughter, maybe cut her from her crotch to her throat, how about run over her with his car, or gang rape her till she was dead. He knew this was pure fantasy, Sergeant Jones had warned him stay out of New Jersey, and if he was caught over the state line he would woe regret the day he was born.

Dick had been out of prison for about a year, driving in a seedier part of town he spotted a prostitute selling her wares, he had not been with a woman in four years, pulling to the curb he called out to the prostitute,"How are you doin, need a ride?"She walked to the passenger side of the car, and gave the spiel."Twenty bucks for a blow, and fifty for a screw.""Blow but lets not do it here, I have a place we can go that's more isolated, I will bring you back."

She climbed into the car, Dick pulled from the curb slowly, and drove to an abandoned block of buildings that were bordered by a city dump, and parked.

He let her start to practice her trade, and as she was really getting into it, he grabbed her by by the throat, and pulling a sap struck her three times in the head,the rage he had internalized for four years had nearly driven him nuts, the rage all came out he became a Jekyll and Hyde swearing ,and cursing his voice became low and guttural while holding the prostitute by the throat. He sounded demented, pulled her from the car made sure he had her purse dragged the body to the edge of the dump, stripped off her clothes, and finding a two by four laying in the muck began to beat her till his arms were numb,he   dropped the broken wood in the garbage. Dick looked at his hands they were shaking, and covered in blood."I have to get out of here, if I'm caught they will give me the chair, or life if I'm lucky."

Dick staggered back to the car making sure he had all of her belongings purse, clothes. He started the car and pulled away from the dump, leaving her for dead. He had to stop his hands from trembling, or the cops would think he was drunk, he finally had his revenge albeit on a surrogate. Arriving at his apartment he showered, took his clothes to the local laundry, and washed the blood out of them.

CHAPTER FOURTEEN

BETRAYAL

Across the river Sammy was keeping the FBI, and State Police appraised of the drug trade. Big Lou, one of the made men, picked up the phone on the first ring, all he heard was,"This is Johnny, we need to talk at the usual place. The caller hung up.

Big Lou walked into the pool hall, and glanced at the bar keep who nodded towards the stairs he climbed the stairs, and Johnny was waiting sipping a beer. He looked over at Johnny."So what's the big fucking news, you ruined my dinner?""I was called to a robbery a few months ago, when we arrived this big Polack comes out of the store flashing a badge, and Sammy was laying on the store floor handcuffed. We were told to forget everything that it's the FBI's bust, and keep our mouths shut. It's taken me six months, but I finally put the make on the cop. He's a State Cop from up north, he was the plant on the dredge when the drug bust went down. Sammy disappeared for over a week, and all of a sudden Sammy shows up like nothing ever happened. I think, he was turned, and is a plant in the organization."

Lou just listened, thinking back on the last couple of raids, Sammy was always somewhere else, and had the information to alert the Feds.

Lou just waved to Johnny, signaling shut up, and get out, he walked down the stairs, went behind the bar picked up the phone dialed, and had a very short conversation, then hung up.

Sammy lay in bed with his latest squeeze, it was three in the morning, the phone was ringing off the hook,"Sammy this is Jerry, we have a job to do", Big Lou's orders.

Sammy whines,"For Christ's sake it's three in the morning."

"It comes from the top, I'll meet you in front of your place in twenty minutes." Jerry answers.

Sammy was waiting at the curb when Jerry pulled up, he jumped into the passenger seat, never noticing that someone occupied the rear seat, Jerry gunned the car" and halfway down the block there was a loud "Pop", Sammy slumped forward, his head hitting the dash.

Jerry hollered,"Jesus, I thought you were going to take him out when we parked?"Tony just grinned,"Wanted to make sure we were safe, he could have been carrying."

"Now, I have to clean up this frigging car, his brains are all over the dashboard."Jerry groaned."Will you shut up, and drive to the river."Tony answered.

When they arrived at the river, they dragged Sammy's corpse out of the car Tony,"Pull down his pants."He put on a pair of surgical gloves, snorted a line of coke reached down, and with one cut had Sammy's manhood in his hand. He tossed the scalpel to Jerry,"Now cut out his tongue."

This being completed, Tony took Sammy's appendage, and stuck it in his mouth, they carried the body to the river, and heaved him in, Tony looked at Jerry,"We want him to be found, it will make anyone who even thinks of being a snitch, will think twice, because if anyone gets caught squealing this is what happens to them."

REBIRTH

After the trial Brenda and her daughter Sara moved to western Ohio and started a new life, Brenda remarried, had two children by her second husband, a boy and a girl. She never saw Dick again.

Dick had been living in the apartment for fifteen years he sat looking out his second story window, watching the people, and traffic in silence. He had aged thirty years, and turned into a wizened old man.

It was a bright sunny day, his sister had just left groceries. Dick poured himself a glass of whisky, as he raised it to his lips, he felt a sudden shock. The glass fell from his hand, and he sat staring out the window for a long, long time.

www.ingramcontent.com/pod-product-compliance
Lightning Source LLC
Chambersburg PA
CBHW031035190726
48286CB00003BA/1183